W9-COI-154

DATE DUE

AUG 7 1973	SEP 12 1980	FE
AUG 23 1973	DEC 29 1980	OC 13 '88
SEP 6 1973	OCT. 7 1981	MY 14 '90
SEP 22 1973	FEB. 22 1982	JE 7 '90
OCT 15 1973	MAR. 25 1982	AG 9 '90
NOV 3 1973	SEP. 23 1982	JA 24 '91
JUL 4 1974	OCT. 28 1982	JY 25 '91
JUL 23 1974	DEC. 1 1982	NO 27 '92
JUL 30 1974	JAN. 25 1983	JY 12 '93
FEB 18 1975	MAR. 15 1983	JUN 27 '95
SEP 1 1975	JAN 30 1983	MAR 28 '96
FEB 10 1976	MAR 30 1983	JUN 26 '96
FEB 25 1976	JUL 7 1983	MAR 28 '97
MAR 1 1976	SEP. 9 1983	MAY 08
MAR 27 1976	OCT 24 1983	JY 10 '02
JUN 1 1976	JUL 06 1984	MY 0
JUL 24 1980	JY 23 '85	AG NO 15
		AG 08

DEMCO 38-297

10,804

Barr, Catherine
Peppy of Portugal

EAU CLAIRE DISTRICT LIBRARY

PEPPY
OF PORTUGAL

BY CATHRINE BARR

HENRY Z. WALCK, INC.   **NEW YORK**

Copyright © 1971 by Catherine Barr. All rights reserved. ISBN: 0-8098-1182-0. Library of Congress Catalog Number: 72-158861. Printed in the United States of America.

EAU CLAIRE DISTRICT LIBRARY

70209

10,804

DEDICATED TO HOPE BLAIR

2

"Oh, Peppy, you aren't useful."
Manuel spoke to his burro as they
ran together to Fernando's house.

Manuel panted to Fernando, his
best friend, "Papa says ———I can't
keep Peppy ——— if he doesn't
earn some money."

Where in all of Portugal could
such a small burro earn money?

"Hey, Peppy can help the oxen pull the boats at Nazaré. Today! We'll go with Uncle Carlos in his truck. Hurry!"

They rushed with Peppy into the back of Uncle Carlos's truck.

"Manuel, look at those tiny legs.
How can Peppy help the oxen?"

"Fernando, you know his heart is stout."

After hours of
bouncing along, the
truck stopped at
Nazaré. Peppy jumped
out and trotted to the
beach ahead of the boys.

"See him go! Is he ever frisky!"

Peppy didn't even look as he
charged along.

7

Wham! Right into a line of clean
clothes hung to dry on the beach.
Down came the line, clothes dragging
in the sand.

The laundress screamed at Peppy,

who ran faster than ever.

Manuel and Fernando ran faster too,
but they couldn't catch Peppy.

The burro dashed by a woman lifting
her basket of fish.

He kicked up his heels and sent her
fish flying.

"Sorry," called the boys as they sped
past the angry woman.

"Wait, Peppy!" Peppy flicked his ears.

"Wait!" And the burro did wait.

"Behave now!" said Manuel right in the burro's fuzzy ear. He tied a rope around Peppy's little shoulders.

"You must work with the oxen."

Down the beach a fishing boat was
coming in. Manuel and Fernando
hurried to be there with Peppy.

"My burro will help your oxen," offered Manuel to the boss.

"Aaaah, what can he do?" asked the boss. "We need strength."

"His heart is stout," promised Manuel,
again and again. And the boss
finally agreed to let Peppy help.

The burro was tied with the
huge oxen. They all pulled at
the heavy boat, straining together
to bring it onto the sand.

But the work was slow. Suddenly
Peppy whirled about and pulled
very hard in the opposite direction.

"Yi-yi!" roared the boss, cutting
Peppy loose. "You are a nuisance.
Get out of here!"

Peppy snatched the boss's cap
right from his head as he ran off.

The boys were scared. They
chased after the burro.
What a relief to see
Uncle Carlos coming with
his truck. They scrambled
aboard, pulling Peppy
with them.

But Manuel didn't want to
go home. Peppy hadn't proved
he could earn money.

"That donkey's just no good," said
Uncle Carlos. And he drove back to
Sintra, where Fernando lived.

At Fernando's house his little
sister, Maria, was playing in the
yard with two friends.

Maria was sitting in a new
cart. Her little friends were trying
to pull it. They tugged and tugged.

It wouldn't budge.

Manuel and Fernando ran from the truck with Peppy.

"Hey," called Fernando. "That's the place for Peppy."

Hooray! Peppy pulled the cart.
Maria squealed. Her friends clapped.
The boys cheered. Peppy brayed.

Each one had a ride in turn.
Proudly Peppy pulled the cart.

Every day, after that, Peppy took many children
for rides, and earned many centavos.

Did Papa let Manuel keep Peppy?
Of course.